For the Montoyas

VIKING
An imprint of Penguin Random House LLC, New York

First published in the United States of America by Viking,
an imprint of Penguin Random House LLC, 2021

LIBRARY OF CONGRESS CATALOGING-IN-PUBLICATION DATA IS AVAILABLE.

Manufactured in China

ISBN 9780593117668

1 3 5 7 9 10 8 6 4 2

The art for this book was made using charcoal, crayon, pencil, and cut paper,
then colored digitally.

NO PANTS!

Jacob Grant

VIKING

Time to wake up, Pablo.
Today is a special day.

Yes! Party Day!

That's right, the whole family
will be at the cookout today.
But first, breakfast!

Pancakes, please!

There's not enough time
for pancakes.
We're having oatmeal.   Um. OK.

Did you put your bowl
in the sink?
Yes.

And brush your teeth?
Yes.

Use the potty?
Yes.

Wash your hands?
Yes.

OK, Pablo, just get dressed and
we'll be ready to go.

Pablo, we can't go
to the party if you
don't put on
your pants.

I don't need pants to party.

You have to wear pants, Pablo.
It's what we do when we go outside.
Everybody wears pants.

Everybody?

Cousin Marco wears pants
on the basketball court.
Aunt Margaret wears pants
in the mountains.

The Montoyas wear
pants to every recital.
And Grandpa . . .

Does not wear pants!
NO PANTS!

Maybe not all of the time, Pablo, but most people wear pants some of the time.

Yoga teachers wear yoga pants.

Firefighters wear turnout pants.

Surgeons wear scrub pants.

Even Grandpa wears sweatpants. Sometimes.

But not all the time.

And pants have been around long before
Grandpa was born! Pants have been made
in every shape and size you can imagine,
and people wear pants all around the
planet. Even in space!

Now, please get dressed, Pablo. We don't
want to be late for the party.

Any pants I can imagine?

Could I wear pants
like this?

Or are they better
like this?

Upside down pants
are the best pants!

Pablo, nobody wears pants
like that.

If everybody wears pants, maybe Waffles
should wear pants too!

Maybe all animals should wear pants!

Pants for cats and dogs and bears
and . . .

WHOOPS!

Enough, Pablo!
Just. Put. On.
Something!
We need to
leave for the
party now.

But where are **your** pants?

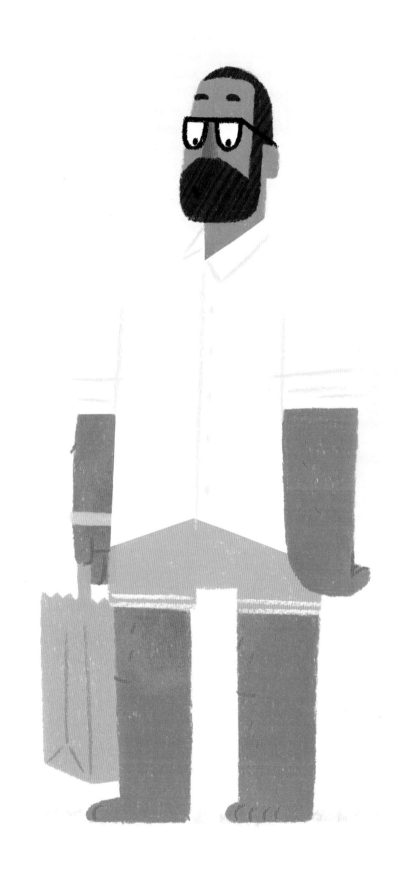

The party may have started, but there's nothing wrong with being fashionably late!

NO PANTS!